Don't Eat The Bluebonnets

Written by
Ellen Leventhal
& Ellen Rothberg

Illustrated by
Bill Megenhardt

ISBN# 978-0-9645493-3-3
LOC Control# 2006923084

Ellen Leventhal -- [1951-]
Ellen Rothberg -- [1956-]
Bill Megenhardt -- [1958-]
    Don't Eat The Bluebonnets / by Ellen Leventhal and Ellen Rothberg
    Illustrator Bill Megenhardt -- 1st ed.
    p.cm.
    SUMMARY: Sue Ellen eats all the bluebonnets and must solve the
    problem of getting them to come back the next spring.
    Audience: Ages 3-8.
    ISBN 978-0-9645493-3-3 (hardback with jacket)
    1. Nature -- Juvenile Fiction. 2. Problem Solving -- Juvenile Fiction.
    3. Consequences -- Juvenile Fiction.].Title.

Bluebonnets, Boots & Books
11010 Hanning Lane
Houston, TX 77041-5006
713-937-9184

www. BluebonnentsBootsandBooks.com

Illustrations & Cover Design — Bill Megenhardt
Book Packager — Rita Mills of the Book Connection
www.bookconnectiononline.com
Editor — Kathi Appelt

The paper used in this publication meets the requirements of the American National
Standard for Permanence of Paper for Printed Library Materials Z39.48-1984.

Printed in Hong Kong

For a cow Sue Ellen had a mind of her own. When the other cows mooed, Sue Ellen whistled. When Max, the Longhorn, gave an order, all the cows snapped to attention—except Sue Ellen. She just swished her tail, batted her lashes, and smelled the daisies.

Every spring Max puts up a sign
in Sue Ellen and Lisa Jean's favorite pasture.

"Humph," Sue Ellen said. "Max is not the boss of me.
He can't tell me what to do." With that she hooked
tails with Lisa Jean and they sashayed across the field.

"I can eat the bluebonnets if I want to," she snorted.

"The bluebonnets won't come back next spring if you eat
them," Lisa Jean warned.

"But we eat the grass, and it comes back," Sue Ellen argued.

"That's true," replied Lisa Jean, "but bluebonnets are
different. They won't come back."

Having a mind of her own, Sue Ellen wasn't totally convinced. The next day when Sue Ellen and Lisa Jean arrived at the south pasture, the bluebonnets were just starting to pop up. Sue Ellen's mouth watered.

"Don't forget. We're not supposed to eat the bluebonnets," Lisa Jean reminded her.

"I'm not eating them. I'm just looking at them," Sue Ellen said, licking her lips.

As they stood beside the pond, Sue Ellen stuck her nose in the air and took a deep breath. "Don't the bluebonnets smell yummy?"

"Don't eat the bluebonnets," Lisa Jean reminded her.

Sue Ellen licked her lips again. "I'm not eating them. I'm just smelling them." She swished her tail. "Water comes back to the pond every year, doesn't it?" she muttered.

Later as Sue Ellen and Lisa Jean were grazing in the shade of the big oak tree, Sue Ellen noticed one small, perfect bluebonnet. It looked delicious. Her mouth watered.

"Don't eat the bluebonnets," Lisa Jean reminded her.

Sue Ellen stuck her tongue out and licked the perfect flower. "I'm not eating it. I'm just licking it."

She looked up at the trees and swished her tail. "The leaves on the trees come back every year, don't they?" she said. "So do the birds," said Sue Ellen as they watched the mockingbirds teach their babies to fly.

"I guess they do," Lisa Jean said as she watched each baby leave the nest and return safely.

By the end of the week the bluebonnets covered the pasture and Sue Ellen couldn't stop thinking about them. She imagined how the petals would taste sliding down her throat. Sue Ellen thought about the water in the pond, she remembered the leaves coming back every spring, and she watched the birds fly by. And with that she charged into the south pasture and ate every single bluebonnet.

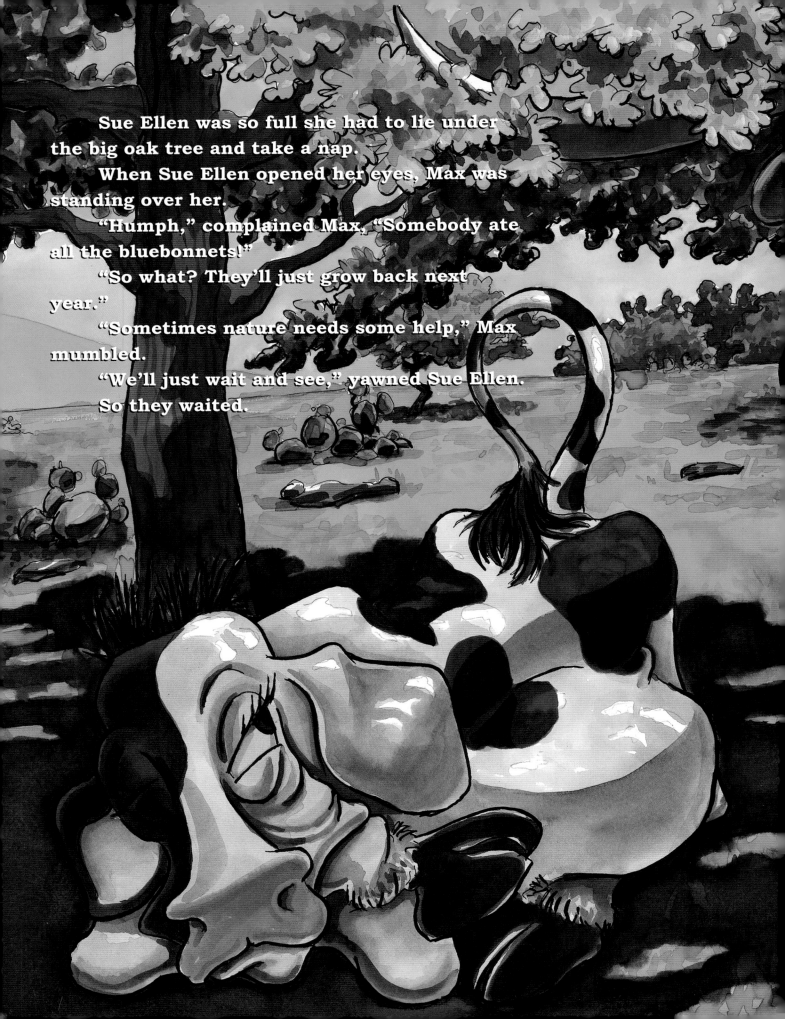

Sue Ellen was so full she had to lie under the big oak tree and take a nap.

When Sue Ellen opened her eyes, Max was standing over her.

"Humph," complained Max, "Somebody ate all the bluebonnets!"

"So what? They'll just grow back next year."

"Sometimes nature needs some help," Max mumbled.

"We'll just wait and see," yawned Sue Ellen.

So they waited.

The spring faded.

The summer came and went.

In the fall the leaves fell.

The winter chill blew in from the north.

Sue Ellen and Lisa Jean thought spring would never come. Then the days began to grow longer and the snow started to melt.

When the spring grass grew so tall that it tickled their bellies, they knew it was time to head to the south pasture where the bluebonnets grew.

When they reached the pasture that morning, they saw Max carrying his sign.

"Well, Sue Ellen, I guess we won't be needing this sign since the bluebonnets haven't grown back," Max bellowed.

All the cows glared at Sue Ellen.

Having a mind of her own, Sue Ellen decided to take charge. "If the bluebonnets won't come back," she thought, "I'll bring them back myself." With that she swished her tail and headed to the north pasture to gather some of the bluebonnets growing there. "Bluebonnets are bluebonnets," she said. "I'll just move the bluebonnets from the north pasture to the south pasture."

By midday the bluebonnets had wilted and were so flat that even the bees couldn't find the pollen in them.

Having a mind of her own, Sue Ellen decided to take charge. "Bluebonnets are bluebonnets. I'll just paint them on the hay," she thought as she grabbed her paints.

As Sue Ellen finished painting the last bale of hay, she glanced up and exclaimed in shock, "Well, that isn't going to work for long!"

Having a mind of her own, Sue Ellen didn't give up. She took her paints, scissors, construction paper, and glue and headed to the south pasture. By the end of the day the field was alive with paper bluebonnets that Sue Ellen had made herself.

That night, a Texas size thunderstorm woke Sue Ellen up. Lightening lit up the sky, the thunder boomed, and the rain soaked the ground.

When Sue Ellen and Lisa Jean got to the pasture the
next morning, the paper bluebonnets had blown away.
"I guess only real bluebonnets are the blue of the
sky. And only real bluebonnets have that wonderful smell.
And only real bluebonnets are worth licking," she sighed.

So, having a mind of her own, Sue Ellen decided to take charge. That night she went to the south pasture and planted a packet of Max's seeds she had found in the barn.

When the next spring came, Sue Ellen took out her paints and freshened up Max's sign.

"Max," she said, batting her lashes, "Will you please put the sign up again?"

He laughed. "There's no need. The bluebonnets won't be back."

It wasn't long before their favorite pasture was beautiful again.
Having a mind of her own, Sue Ellen decided she could
. . . look at the bluebonnets
. . . smell the bluebonnets
. . . lick the bluebonnets. . .

but she could not eat the bluebonnets.

Books and the First Amendment have long been a passion of **Rita Mills** so it is only natural that her career change in the early '90s would be from newspapers to publishing books. Don't Eat the Bluebonnets is the twentieth children's picture book that she has shepherded in her career and she hopes there are many more in her future. Rita lives in Houston, Texas and manages to keep busy with her work, her daughter and two sons, and eight grandchildren.

Ellen Rothberg wrote and illustrated her first children's book with a friend at the age of 7, and although she no longer draws the pictures, she still likes to write with her friend, Ellen Leventhal. She is a former elementary school teacher and is currently at work on a master's degree in school counseling. She lives in Houston, Texas with her husband. She and her husband both love cows, bluebonnets and their two college-age children.

While growing up in New Jersey, **Ellen Leventhal** didn't dream of bluebonnet fields, but she did dream of writing books. Ellen has a master's degree in education and has been writing for and with her students for many years. She has lived in Houston, Texas with her husband for over twenty years and is the proud mother of two grown sons, who love bluebonnets, Longhorns, and just about anything Texan.

Bill Megenhardt has drawn pictures ever since he can remember. He is an illustrator living in Houston, Texas with his son Michael.

Authors' Notes

Every year in Texas, people from El Paso to Dallas, Lubbock to Austin, and all points in between excitedly await the first sign of spring . . . a blanket of bluebonnets. Whether they're on hills, beside highways, or in a cow's pasture, bluebonnets symbolize Texas as much as ten-gallon hats, cowboy boots, and Longhorn steers. Although there is no specific law protecting bluebonnets, everyone from schoolchildren to groundskeepers know the importance of preserving nature, so although you may look at the bluebonnets, sit among the bluebonnets, and even photograph the bluebonnets, please don't ever pick the bluebonnets.

While cows can eat bluebonnets without harm, they can sometimes be toxic to other animals including humans.

Sue Ellen lives on a ranch in Texas with her little sister Lisa Jean, a herd of other cows, and a longhorn steer named Max. She now looks forward to the spring each year.